# Flying Dolls and Smiling Friends

**Unni Ammayambalam**

*Translation & Illustration by* **Austin Ajit**

**Ukiyoto Publishing**

All global publishing rights are held by

**Ukiyoto Publishing**

Published in 2024

Content Copyright © Austin Ajit

**ISBN 9789361727832**

*All rights reserved.*

*No part of this publication may be reproduced, transmitted, or stored in a retrieval system, in any form by any means, electronic, mechanical, photocopying, recording or otherwise, without the prior permission of the publisher.*

*The moral rights of the author have been asserted.*

*This is a work of fiction. Names, characters, businesses, places, events, locales, and incidents are either the products of the author's imagination or used in a fictitious manner. Any resemblance to actual persons, living or dead, or actual events is purely coincidental.*

*This book is sold subject to the condition that it shall not by way of trade or otherwise, be lent, resold, hired out or otherwise circulated, without the publisher's prior consent, in any form of binding or cover other than that in which it is published.*

www.ukiyoto.com

*To my grandparents and parents, for always supporting and encouraging me.*

# Foreword

**Flying Colours:**

This is the second book of Master Austin Ajit under the category of Translation. Translation is the bridge between two languages, and he has done an exceptional work.

I extend my immense pleasure to be a part of Austin's remarkable literary journey. Either I travel with him, or he is taking me along. Other than his intellectual, informative, and educative previous books, "Flying Doll and Smiling friends " appears to be of simple narrative about everything in general .

But when you look at it, this book is also an educative book covering all primary lessons for kids and for elders, something to ponder about the good Samaritans.

This exquisite book gives the reader an amazing feeling of bliss, living in the midst of only positivity. It's all about animals, birds and humans living in harmony in the green pastures of life without affecting the negatives of today's world.

The story begins with a "Chinese whisper" of guessing about the weird creature sitting on the wall by whatsoever imbecile, haughty animals and portent birds! But they never intent any harm each other.

As soon as they realise that it is a winged doll and that it's the mission is to find her lost mother, it takes life and enter the reader's heart! The beauty is that the doll's wings will activate when it becomes happy and laughs. After that as the animals help her to find Minikutty, she is also entering as a naive smiling girl.

Austin's imagination also flies with the Doll and the reader honestly becomes a part of everything by joining in searching for the Doll's mother. The story is almost like a play with songs, and it is omniscient! The book covers from rhyming words to acrostic poems, cries of animals, bird's nests etc . It teaches the kids all about vegetables, its colour, uses and vitamins.

As the Doll flies with Minikutty the narrative is like a beautiful picture from above. Other than spreading the message of love and care, the flying Doll leaves a message of sacrifice of own happiness for other less fortunate like the nomads. Good deeds will be rewarded, and the Doll gets boons from the Sun and the Moon! The book gives you a beautiful feeling altogether.

I am so happy and proud to pen an appreciation note for Austin's work who has done it with flying colours with golden tint. I congratulate the author and the little translator ,Master Austin Ajit .

All the best wishes little author Austin in the line of writing which is your favourite field!!

**BRIJI .K.T :** Bilingual writer and artist. Published many books including books for children by Kerala Gov. "Institute for children's literature. "In the platform of art , I have conducted several exhibitions including in Bangalore Chithra Kala Parishath. Won many awards including international Muse award for Poetry ,and "women achievers award " 2020.

# Contents

| | |
|---|---:|
| A flying leopard? | 1 |
| The doll's destination | 7 |
| Minikutty's house | 10 |
| Lets rock! | 18 |
| Where has the doll flew to? | 21 |
| Fly, doll, fly! | 23 |
| A trip to Granny's house | 27 |
| Granny talks about of the mama doll. | 32 |
| The search for Mama doll in the garden | 34 |
| Tomatoes and his friends | 40 |
| The story of sacrifice | 45 |
| What happened next? | 49 |
| *About the Author* | *50* |

# A flying leopard?

"Guys! Look over there, at that animal! It is sitting on top of the wall…menacingly. It has red wings, sparkling eyes, and a white, black, and yellow body!

The goat, the cow, the puppy, the hen, the crow, and the cat took a step back, before peeking carefully at the mysterious creature. But, in their fear, they tip-toed backwards again. "What is that thing? It looks like a leopard!" said the cat.

"Do leopards have wings?Don't tell foolish things" Replied the goat.

"When you see it from far away it resembles a tiger cub. When there are tiger cubs, a mother tiger will always be nearby… I'm SO SCARED! I don't want to be eaten by a tiger!" said the cow, shivering in fright.

"Do tigers have wings also? You imbeciles!" said the goat haughtily.

The puppy got tired of hearing the goat's arrogant replies and said "Hey goat! This is a time where massive changes are happening to all kinds of animals, including tigers. My mother told me that a two headed tiger was born once!".

"If that's so, then this has to be a tiger cub!" said the cow, shivering. "It's sitting on the wall and planning how to jump and eat us all!"

The crow got an idea. He asked whether he should fly and look at the mysterious creature up close, but then the hen said "No, you should not. We should tip-toe away quietly and run for our lives! That is the only way! I know about these foxes. Granny Hen told me that nowadays flying foxes are very common, and that we should keep our eyes peeled for them!". Hen stood, ready to make a run for it.

Just as they were going to run away, Mr squirrel arrived. The friends told everything to him.

"Creature, creature on that wall.

Scary creature on that wall!

Who is sitting on that wall?

Who is scary on that wall!"

"Ha-ha Ha!" laughed Mr Squirrel.


Not knowing why on earth Mr Squirrel was laughing, the other animals said:

"We saw wings, we saw wings.

Not a vulture's, not a crow's

Is it a tiger cub growling?

Or a fox howling?"


Yet again, Mr squirrel laughed. Rolling on his back, he was crying with laughter. His big furry tail and his stubby legs shook as he laughed. "There is no need to worry" he said. "For this is just a doll. A doll with wings!".

The cow, the goat, the puppy, the cat, the crow, and the hen stood, astounded, for this mysterious creature was a flying doll! Not a tiger, not a fox, not at all a leopard, but instead a doll! The goat's mouth felt open, followed by the puppy's and the cow's. "Ha... till now... we were scared by ... that was... a doll?". They stammered, struggling to grip this new information.

"The friends who were scared of the doll laughed hahaah..

The doll without knowing why, joined in haahha.."

They all had a hearty laugh, when the doll's wings stood straight up. Like a majestic aeroplane, the doll flew above the friends, who promptly looked up.

# The doll's destination

"We can dance,

We can dance and sing,

We can sing a tune and play!

Who who who?"

Sang the doll. "Do you like my song friends?" She asked.

The cow and the goat immediately said 'Yes!', followed by the other friends. The doll began flying lower. "Then can you say who am I?" asked the doll.

"A winged doll!" said Mr Squirrel. He rolled in front of the doll, making her smile. She liked seeing the funny way that Mr Squirrel rolled around. "Where are you going, doll?".

The doll replied "far away, into the town. There is a big house in the town where a girl named Minikutty lives. I am going there".

"Singing a song,

I will fly,

I'm a nice little doll,

To make a new friend,

A trip to Minikutty's"

The doll then told the animals to ask why she wanted to make friends with Minikutty. "It is a very sad story… it makes my eyes water to think about it".

She said, "Long ago, me and my mother were living together. That's when Minikutty came. She saw my mother and thought that she looked good. So Minikutty took my mother to play with. I was heartbroken, and on seeing my pain, Chanda Maama (the moon) gave me these wings to fly and find my mama. I could fly across world to save mama doll. When I've found my mama the wings will go away. My mama will be in Minikutty's house, right? Will you all help me?"

"Definitely!" said everyone at the same time. "Minikutty is our friend! She comes here time to time. She comes to stay in her grandpa's house," said cat. "Now fly towards the east, where you will find a mango tree. There you will find Minikutty's house. Nearby you should see Kunjuettan's shop." Said the goat. The doll nodded. "Ok, now go! Save your mother!" encouraged the cat. But the doll shook her head and said, "I can only fly when I laugh!". The friends said "oh, that's cool! We shall sing a song. Then you will get the power to fly."

"Bow wow

Bow wow,

Kuttee made coffee,

For Kitu he made coffee,

The glass broke,

So spilled the coffee,

Kitu got no coffee".

Sang the puppy. The doll laughed, and her wings began flapping like a helicopter at the same time. She flew up and looked at the friends. They looked back and prayed that the doll would succeed in her mission. "let the doll find her mother"…

## Minikutty's house

After flying for many hours; with a huge, tired, sigh; the doll reached Minikutty's house.

A plan popped into her head. *"if I sit in front of Minikutty's door and wait, she will surely open the door and see me! She will hold me and kiss me, and then take me inside. After all, who doesn't like a good doll!"*.

A small shop in Pattam,

A nearby house,

To forge a friendship with a girl,

Waits a doll.


***"It's pretty early in the morning, but Minikutty should get up now"*** thought the doll. She hears Minikutty's voice talking inside. She was saying good morning to her parents. **"I'll be quiet. Let this be a surprise! Wait a minute... she's coming! Straight here!"**

Let my dear Minikutty

My adorable Minikutty

come,

A doll awaits!


Minikutty opened the door. The early morning sun cast yellow shadows all over the place. The rays of light were drying up the dew laden grass. Just as she was about to go back, she saw a doll. "hey! What a cool doll! It looks so beautiful! With wide eyes, red wings, and tiger stripes... I love this doll already!". Minikutty hugged and kissed the doll.


A round-eyed doll,

A wide-eyed doll,

A cutie-pie doll,

A magic flying doll!.

*'I'll take this doll inside. My parents will love it at first sight! They will stare at its beauty.'* thinks Minikutty. "So doll, shall we go inside?" she asks.

Saying this, Minikutty takes the doll on her shoulder, walks inside and closed the door. The doll thinks *' Oh! I'm going inside now! I don't know whether Minikutty's parents will like me... I'll have to stay here for a while. Maybe my mama will be here only! I will have to search everywhere.'.*

The doll was thinking and planning, when Minikutty plopped her onto the table. She said "Doll, will you please sit here and wait for me? I have neither brushed my teeth nor have I freshened up. You don't have to do any of those things, do you?'. Minikutty's mother called from the kitchen. "Who are you talking to this early in the morning Minikutty?". Minikutty responded 'come here! I want to show you and father something!" Her mother and father came and asked "Whose doll is this? Where did you find it?". Minikutty said "I found it outside our doorstep". Mother and father said that it might be one of the neighbouring kid's toys, but Minikutty said "No, they do not have this kind of wonderful doll. Let it be here, I'll freshen up and come. After all, I have to go to school today, right?". Singing a song, she went to brush here teeth.

After you get up every morning,

It's neat to brush your teeth!

Then eat some yummy breakfast

So you get plenty of energy

 And don't fall asleep!


The doll let out a huge, tired sight. *'I think Minikutty's parents both liked me! Minikutty's mother is working in the kitchen, and is being helped by Minikutty's father. How nice this house is ! How beautiful this living room is! There are books, toys and dolls; all stacked and kept neatly! There are sofas and vases, paintings and more!'* The doll looked around. *'If I was a kid then I would walk and explore everything. Hmm… will my mama be in the toy closet? There's a cat there staring at me from the shelf!'.*

There's a closet; a toy closet,

With a kitty cat- a toy cat,

Inside the closet,

Filled with toy rats, bats and hats,

Buses and bees that buzzes ,

Toys that shine and glow,

Looking so beautiful!


The doll looked and looked, but there was no sign of her mama. Suddenly a     -SSSS- sound alerted her. The doll looked around and saw that the sound came from the kitchen. It was Minikutty's mother making a dosa. The doll turned back and got an idea. '*I can peek at all the cupboards and shelfs.*'

Inside the kitchen,

Inside the kitchen,

What is, what is inside the kitchen?

Glasses that shine!

Spoons covered in grime!

Bowls and plates,

And an item that grates!

Shining beautifully.

16   Flying dolls and Smiling friends

But in the kitchen also the dolls mama was not there. By that time, Minikutty had come. She said "Look mother! I'm all ready to go!". Her mother replied by saying "Dosa and chutney is ready! Come quickly and call your brother too". Minikutty replied "Brother is studying. He wants to come first place in the exam. I'll try to call him." Minikutty called him and he finally came to the living room. "Ahh, what a nice doll!" He spoke. The doll got very happy, while Minikutty got even happier! She said "After school me and the doll and my friends are going to play. We are going to rock!". Brother said "I'll come to play too!". Minikutty said "If you are also coming then we will jump, run and play! But don't say that you lost your first place in the exam because of us." "Ok, ok!" laughed her brother.

# Lets rock!

KNOCK KNOCK! Someone was knocking at the door. Minikutty's mother called. "Minikutty! Just check who is knocking at the door?". Minikutty, who has just came back from school, ran and checked. "It's Muhammad!" Muhammad was Minikutty's neighbour and friend. He saw the doll and and said "Wow! What a nice doll!" Minikutty said that it was her doll. Muhammad said " Let us go play with this doll. Come on!". Minikutty said " I just came from school! At least give me a minute to freshen up and come!". In response, Muhammad snatched the doll and ran. "MOTHER! Muhammad took my doll and is running away!" yelled Minikutty. Mother said " He probably took it to play. You run after him and play!". Minikutty ran after him, shouting " MUHAMMAD! STOP!". Muhammad says " Come, come!". Minikutty replies " Unni, Uma, Roni, Chinju and me! We all are coming!".

Soon all the children saw the doll, and at once said "Wow! A doll with wings! Red wings!" Roni asked whether he could poke it. Unni wanted to play with it. Minikutty pushed past them all, saying " Don't rip or tear it!". The children launched into a song.

A beautiful doll,

Wings red as roses,

And colours as vibrant as rainbows,

This is our doll!

And it's an epic doll.

The doll was terrified as all the children pulled and dragged her. Each one wanted the doll for themselves. Suddenly, Minikutty pointed at the sky and said "LOOK! A PARROT!"

A bright green parrot

Who loves eating carrots.

A big red beak

And big chubby cheeks!

Suddenly, a "COCKADOODLE DOO" emerged from behind the wall. Minikutty says " Maybe the rooster came to save the doll from being torn apart! The children sing now about a rooster.

A big, fat rooster,

Waits as the sun comes closer,

Climbing higher into the sky.

COCKADOODLE DOO!

He yells, telling everyone what to do.

It's time to wake up, the sun has risen!

So says the rooster, so we better listen.

Hearing this song, the doll laughed. And when the doll laughs, her wings activate! Thus, her wings stand straight. ZOOM! The doll flies away, in rocket speed. At first, Minikutty and her friends laugh. After all, seeing a doll flying like a rocket is really funny! But then realisastion dawns upon them. The doll had gone! *"Will this doll come back?'* wonders everyone.

# Where has the doll flew to?

Now, after a while, the doll came back. Everyone played for a while, before they all went home. Minikutty and her brother went to sleep;They were tired yet happy. " That was fun, right? We played all day long!" said Minikutty. Her brother replied " Yeah! It was awsome! I'm so tired though". Minikutty said " I'm going to hug my doll and sleep.". Brother said " Don't hug the doll too tightly, or it will fly away!". " Don't make fun, me and the doll are best friends! Come doll, let us sleep!".

Soon after Minikutty slept, the doll got up. She quietly whispered. *"Minikutty? Are you awake?"*. Minikutty was in a deep sleep, and didn't even notice. The doll got up and flew everyewhere, searching in all the cupboards and closets and doors. She looked everywhere, but she didn't see what she was looking for: Her mama. Feeling sad, she fell down nearby Minikutty. THUD! Minikutty woke up with a start, and seeing the doll crying, she asked " Why are you crying?". The tearful doll told her the story of her mama doll, and Minikutty felt sad. She said " No need to cry, I kept it here safley in a closet". The doll asked " Safley? IN WHICH CLOSET?".

Minikutty kept quiet for a while, but seeing the dolls disraught face, she told " Ok, listen. There is a way to see your mother doll.". " HOW?" aksed the doll. "You are a flying doll, right? You can take me on your back and fly outside. I will show you where your mother is!" The doll felt scared about flying in the dark, but upon hearing that she could see her mother again, the doll instantly agreed. Thus, Minikutty and the doll flew outside into the cold, dark night.

# Fly, doll, fly!

Minikutty admired the scenery. " The moon is so nearby that if I strech out a bit I can touch it! The stars are all smiling and laughing. See the beauty! Such nice cool breeze too!. The doll agreed, for it was beautiful.

Like a green blanket,

Lies rows of paddyfields.

Like a tiny shrub,

Are all the trees and herbs.

Like ants are the elephants,

Like pebbles are the hills,

Everything seems small,

When you're high up in the clouds!

Minikutty was brimming with joy. " There are so many houses! Mushroom like ones, stacked box like ones, wide ones, short ones, tall ones! All the cars look like matchboxes! Its becoming early morning, and everyone is getting up".

"You said that we were going to see my mama" said the doll. " We have been flying for hours and I'm so tired!". " Ok, ok" replied Minikutty. " You see that big tree over there? Nearby the river? Fly over to there".

Thus, they flew and landed on the tree. They sat in a small hollow. The doll's wings were tired from flying, and she was happy to take a break. A nice cool breeze came from the river. "This is so nice!" said the doll. Minikutty agreed and said " Do you know what all are in this tree?". The doll replied " Some branches and leaves". Minikutty shook her head and said " No! Look carefully.. on the big, big branches there are many types of hanging bird nests. Do you know what kinds of bird nests these are?". The doll felt irritated, but she did not know that Minikutty was asking these questions in order to make the doll forget about her sadness! The doll looked around and saw no one was nearby. She thought *'Minikutty brought me here to find my mama, so its best that I agree with everything she says.'*. Thinking this, the doll says " I know all of these birdnests."

'The common tailor bird tailors leaves to make a nest,

While the lazy parrakeet uses readymade tree hollows,

The weaver bird weave using threads,

While the kingfishers use mud tunnels,

And the crow uses twigs'.

" Exellent song!" congratualtes Minikutty. " So many birds flying in the sky in the early morning, looking so beautiful!" said the doll. Minikutty nodded her head, agreeing. "Butterflies have colourful wings, parrots have green dresses, crows have a black suit and herons have white shirts! Different birds, different colours and different nests!" says Minikutty. " There are so many proverbs related to birds". " I know, my mama taught me some" says the doll. " Ok, tell me some!" says Minikutty.

"Ok, here is one : A crow will not become a stork by taking a bath" says the doll. " Here is another proverb " Even a crow thinks it's baby is golden".

Minikutty said " Good job!". She clapped her hands, and all the birds flew away. The doll watched the birds an realised that it had became morning time! " Look! It has became morning. Where is my mama doll? Only if we find her can we go back." Said the doll. Minikutty said " Once when I came for a picnic I left the mama doll under the tree. I fell asleep then, and when I woke up I was back at my house. Maybe Granny took it to her house". " Ok then, let us go there!" says the doll.

# A trip to Granny's house

Minikutty and the doll flew until they reached Granny's house.

Minikutty says " look! I'm jumping and coming!" She jumped down from the doll's back and sang " Jumping, singing I shall come! Hungry, tired I shall come!". Granny looked outside and said " Hey! Look who came! My darling Minikutty! You came so early in the morning by yourself? You should not come by yourself this far, yet you wont listen!" greeted Granny joyfully.

"Granny, I'm very hungry, could I have a dosa?" asks Minikutty. " Sure! you can have dosa and some tea also!" answers Granny. Minikutty used to visit her grandparents houses by herself all the time, but now today she came early. Granny didn't know that Minikutty had came on the back of a doll! Minikutty kept the doll onto a sofa and whispered something into its ear.

Granny asks " Shall I sing a song about dosas?

Dosa, dosa,

All kinds of dosas!

Small small  set dosas,

Big fat Masala dosas!

Onion, chilli , egg dosas,

With a bit of chutney,

Makes them all yummy!

Greengram dosa,

Ragi dosas,

A big white dosa!

That comes in the night,

Who made that dosa?

No one knows,

It is our moon!"


Minikutty smilled at this song, and the doll laughed. Remember what happenes if the it laughs? ZOOM! With a flap of its wings, the doll flew. It began searching the house head to toe. To distract Granny from the doll, Minikutty says " That was an epic song Granny!" Granny smiles and says " are you buttering me dear? Just take that grater please". " Coconut graters have teeth on it's tounge." said Minikutty. " Oh, so you know proverbs?" asks Granny. " Only a few. " replies Minikutty.

Granny begins to quiz Minikutty about proverbs.

"What is white in the day and black in the night?" she asks. Minikutty replies " The sun!".

"When you look into him, you see you." Quizes Granny. This time, Minikutty did not know the answer, so Granny said " Mirror!

Next question: Four legs and a curved tail.". Upon receiving no answer, she says " Dog!".

Minikutty ran and hugged Granny. " Granny, I see lots of vegtables in the kitchen and balloons everywhere. What is special today?" she asks. " It is Grandpa's birthday! You know that, right?" asks Granny. " Yeah, I knew that." Says Minikutty. " Will there be Sadhya in a leaf today?".

" Yes, there will", says Granny.

Yummy ,yummy Idiappam

Crunchy, cruchy Neyyappam;

Vada, Vada ,Uzhunnu Vada

Ada, Ada ,Ela Ada

Sambar, Avial

And Pappadam

Tangy, Tangy Pulissery

Thick yet yummy Erissery"

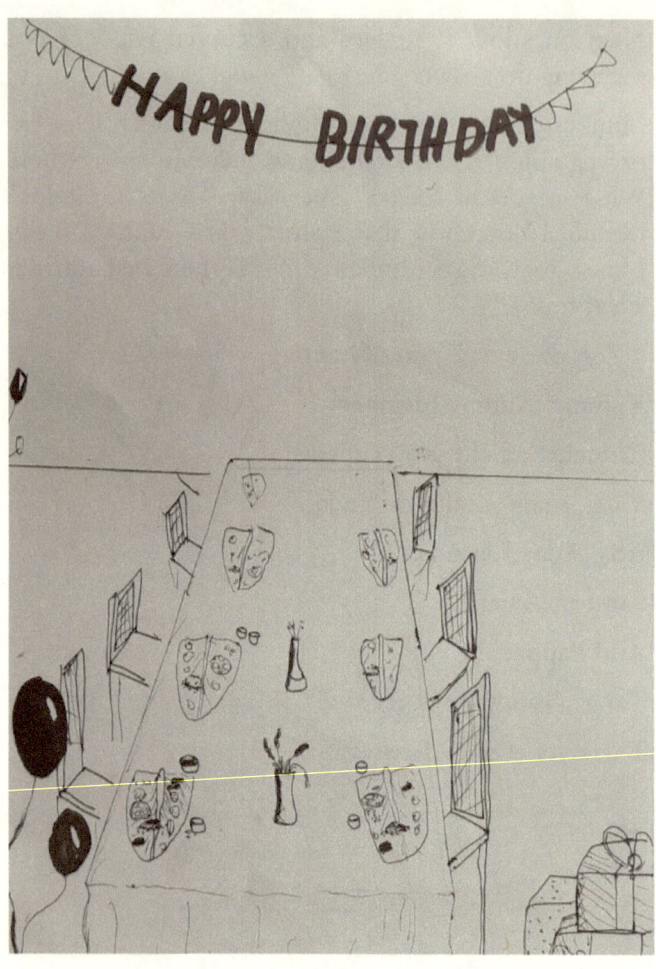

While singing this song, Minikutty remembered: She needed a gift for Grandpa! She began drawing a picture as Granpa's birthday present, when suddenly a call came out. " There is a bird in this room! Come, get a stick!". It was Grandpa. He had found the doll flying everywhere and was going to beat it. Granny came with the stick, and Grandpa was scolding. " Is the house the place to fly a bird?". Minikutty was thinking for a way to save the doll, who was definetly about to be thrased, when an idea struck her!

# Granny talks about of the mama doll.

BANG! Grandpa got scared at the sound. It was Minikutty popping a balloon. She laughed. Granny, seeing Minikutty laugh, also laughed. Grandpa, not wanting to be left out, also laughed! The doll ran and hid behind a closet while everyone was distracted.

Minikutty ran and saw Grandpa in a new shirt and shorts. She laughed and made fun of him. Jokingly, Grandpa raised his hand as if he was going to punch her when Minikutty showed him her drawing. Grandpa went down and put on his specs, before saying " A big tree, underneath it is a moogoose, and animals. Nice job Minikutty!". " Wait, let me also see" said Granny! " Wow! Big tree in the forest, a goat entering the forest, birds and their nests… You are such a good artisit Minikutty!". Minikutty got up and hugged Grandpa.

Then, seeing many vegetables waiting to be cut and cooked in the kitchen, they went and helped Granny make curry. Minikutty motioned the doll to run and search while the coast was clear. Then, while helping Granny make sambar, she asked " Granny, last time I came I had a big doll. When we went for a picnic I left that doll here and went. Do you know where is that doll?". Granny said " Oh that doll? I took it back here". Minikutty took a sigh in relief, thinking that the mama doll was safe when Granny said " But it is not here now. Last time I saw it, it was in the vegetable garden". Hearing this, the doll ( who was spying from behind a wall) felt like crying. Will she ever find her mama? Noticing this Minikutty went to pacify her. "There there, it will be all right. Your mama will be in the vegetable garden". Then, in the afternoon, they ate Sadhya. " Mmm... This is very tasty!" said Grandpa and Minikutty. Granny laughed, and Minikutty hugged her tightly. She sang:

On a straight, strong bannana leaf,

We will lay rice; everyone come!

For a yummy Sadhya,

Parippu and Pappadam must be present!

Sambar, Avial, Thoran and Pachadi must be there!

Kichadi, Kaalan, Ellisheri have to come!

Mezhukkupuratti, Upperi, Naranga curry, Pulissery.

Inji curry has good taste!

Pal Payasam is awsome!

Let me take the Sadhya,

Everyone shall come and eat it!

# The search for Mama doll in the garden

Minikutty takes the doll from outside the closet (where it was hiding) and walked outside. "Where are we going Minikutty?" it asked. " To the garden. Your mama doll will be there. Plus, Granny and Grandpa will also be in the garden!". The duo walk through the garden when a nice breeze flew by. " Ahh, what a nice breeze!" said Minikutty. " I'll hug you tightly, otherwise I'll get carried away!" replied the doll. " Shall I sing a song about wind?"

'The magical wind,

Keeps us cool,

Sing us a song,

To help us sleep,

With a fragrance,

It comes!'

"Good job, you sang without mistakes!" congratulated the doll.

"Whom are you talking to Minikutty?" asked Granny, who had been watering plants. " I'm talking to my doll!" replied Minikutty. " Ok, will you look at the plants and explore, or will you help us water the garden?" asked Grandpa. "I'll explore. There are lots of vegetables here!" answered Minikutty. " Shall we sing a song about vegetables?" asked Grandpa. " Sure! I'd like to hear your sing" said Minikutty.

" Red as rose Tomatoes

Underground: Potatoes!

Crunchy, orange carrots,

That keep being eaten by parrots!

Bitter gourd, bottle gourd,

And a little ash gourd!

Infinite vegetables in my garden!"


"How was my song?" asked Grandpa. "Very good!" laughed Granny. Grandpa to, laughed. Only Minikutty did not say anything. She could not see the doll's mama, and thought that the mama doll was not here also.

Minikutty felt her eyes water. *'What shall I tell the doll? If I say that she won't find her mama, won't she feel sad? What can I do?'*. The doll saw Minikutty's confused, if not slightly sad face and asked " Whats wrong? What are you thinking about Minikutty?" . " I know you, you're thinking about my mama! I heard last night you asking Granny where is my mama doll, and Granny said that she was here in the garden! I know that my mama will be here only. I'll fly and look everywhere. I'll come back with my mama!". Hearing the doll say this, Minikutty felt tears in her eyes. She felt so bad for the doll. " Today only I'll get my mother" said the doll. "

Will you really? Will you actually find your mama?" asked Minikutty. The doll did not like this question, but she ingnored her angry feeling and said " Yes! Definitly!". "If you have that kind of positivity, you will definitly find her!" said Minikutty. " I will" said the doll. The doll hopped of Minikutty's hand and began searching.

After walking for some time, she saw some figures coming in the distance. "Who is coming?" the doll asked herself.

A group of friends

A little dog barking!

An orange cat meowing!

A tall goat nibbling,

On green grass growing!

A big cow mooing!

A rooster crowing,

A white duck pecking!

*'OH!'* thought the doll. *'It's my old friends who helped me find Minikutty' house.* Seeing her friends, the doll said " Hi guys!". " Bow bow! Hello doll! Found your mama yet" said the dog. " Not yet, but I will find her today!". "Meow! Ok then, shall we all play a game? After all, today you will find your mama!". "Ok! We will sing and play.

Each of us should sing a song with some kind of special thing in it. We must say what that special thing is." Said the goat. He gave an example

"Tongue Twisters twist tongues till they tear". " Meow! I know! All the words begin with 't'!" said the cat. "Woof! I know one!" said the dog.

"Bats with hats get bullied by fat cats riding blue mats.".

Everyone thought for a whiles, until the cat again says " The words rhyme: Bat, hat, fat cat, blue mat… wait. You called me a "fat cat?!".

Now it was doll's turn to sing.

'**D**arling little doll

**O**bviously very nice!

**L**ovely and kind

**L**aughing and smiling'

"Nice song doll!" said the cat. Now the goat sings: "

Goats love leaves

Plucked fresh and green!

The cat loves milk

Especially with cream!

The dog likes bones

(not his own)

And the birds like grains

Giving them healthy brains!

The cow eats everyone's hay

So everyone calls: HEY!'

"Now I want to sing a song" said the cat.

" The sky is blue.

The ocean is too!

Plants are green,

with a leafy gleam!

The sun is yellow.

He's quite a bright fellow!"

sang the cat. Hearing to these song, everyone began laughing and jumping.

The cat, like a teacher, leapt upon a fence post and began dictating: "Does everyone understand what was special about these poems?". The animals shook their heads in unison, so the cat said " In the first example poem given by goat, most of the words begin with the letter 't'. This is called **alliteration**, and it's when multiple words have the same first letter. Another example is 'Orange orang-utans on top of orange trees'. Here, most of the words begins with the letter 'o' , the only exception being 'trees' and 'top'. In the dog's poem, most of the words rhyme, making it a **rhyming poem**. When two words have the same end letters or have the same sounding endings, they are called **rhyming words**!

In the dog's poem, they include bat, cat, fat , hat and mat. Another good example is ' There was a bug who's name was chug. He lived under a rug with his pet pug ( a kind of puppy). He used to swim inside a jug and he gave very good hugs!'. Here, bug, chug, rug, mug, jug and hug rhyme!. In the dolls song, each line begins with one letter of the word 'doll'. The first line begins with 'D', the next with O, the next with L, and the last with another L. This way, the poem's first letters make a word : Doll. This is called an **'acrostic poem'**.

To write an acrostic poem, first write a subject word like this:

'C

A

T'

Then, write down a line beginning with each letter that describes the subject.So :

'Cream is my favourite food,

Adorable and cute,

Talented and wonderful'.

See how every sentence's first letter spells out cat? Now, in the last poem by goat is yet another rhyming poem, as most of its words rhyme."

Thus, the cats magnificent speech ended. The friends blinked in shock for a few minutes, before laughing and walking forward. As they walked among the garden, the doll looked everywhere. '*I had promised to find my mama today*' Thought the doll. '*Where is she?*'. Will the doll find her mother today? Or ever?

# Tomatoes and his friends

Deep inside the vegetable garden, the vegetables began to gather. "Come Yam! Everyone else has arrived! Come on!" called Tomato. "Coming Tomato, coming!" replied the Yam. He huffed and puffed his way to the group. The vegetables began talking to each other; telling jokes and other things. "How's Lady's finger and her family?" asked Pumpkin. "My family and I are doing well! In-between a few insects come and munch on all our leaves, but we're still doing well." Replies Lady's finger. Hearing this, Bitter gourd said "Nowadays even my leaves are being eaten by some insects." . "WE NEED A SOLUTION!" said Lady's finger determinedly. She looked at Tomato and Bitter gourd. " True, we need a solution. That's why we all gathered here, right?" says Tomato.

Till now no one else knew the agenda of the meeting. " We need a king to help solve our problems" said Lady's finger. "Us vegetables grow on climbers, plants or underground. From all these kinds of vegetables we need a king!" says Bitter gourd. Tomato nodded his head, agreeing. Animals and birds have their kings. So why not for vegetables? Egg plant spoke up " So who will be our king?". " Without me, no curries can be made, so I should be king!" said Pumpkin. "No, I am the tallest, so the king should be <u>me</u>!" argued Snake gourd.

The Lady's Finger broke out into a song about her benefits.

'As stiff as a stick

With juicy, rich flesh

With fiber antioxidants,

I am the one and only:

Lady's finger!

And a great taste too!'

"I can do better that that' huffed Tomato.

'The secret ingredient,

In everyone's favourite foods,

The ultimate source of nutrients,

And antioxidants too!

A red, round, shining fruit,

That suits your every need.

The one and only Tomato,

Makes a super tasty feast!'

"Hey, Snake gourd" called Pumpkin. " I am the biggest and you are the tallest. Can't we both be kings?" They asked.

'With out us the sadhya is doomed:

Tasteless, pointless –

Before they can even start, the Bitter gourd interrupts. " be quite, for I am the true king!" he says in a mighty voice.

'I'm a juice,

I'm a snack,

I'm a vegetable!

High to the sky,

With nutrients, fiber and taste!

What a waste, if you don't eat- BITTER GOURD!'

Now the climbers sing.

'We are climbers,

Some with fiber,

Others with vitamins A to Z!'

Not to be outdone, the underground plants sing :

'We grow underground,

To get out of the rain,

Filled with proteins,

To help you out in the day'

Hearing the vegetables singing, a huge herd of goats walked towards them. Behind, a rooster called " COCKADOODLEDOOOOOO!".

Cows, dogs, cats, crows and more were walking behind. "Where are they going Tomato?" asked the Lady's finger. " To the wall" replied the Tomato.

Seeing the goats, a Tomato sang :

" Goats, goats ,white goats.

Goats, goats,black goats,

Mama goats , baby goats,

All kinds of colourful goats,

 munching on leaves; goats, goats!'.

All the animals were walking towards the wall.

"Is it enough if we stand here looking at each other? Who will be the king?" asked the Pumpkin. "Can I say something?" asked the Tomato ." We all are vegetables, we all are equally important. So, I'd say that we don't need a king. After all, we stay stronger together !" . The other vegetables liked this idea and chanted " We shall stand together! We all are one!". Hearing this chant, the doll, cow, cat, dog, crow, chicken and the goat arrived, followed by Minikutty. They were listening to the vegetables when they saw smoke coming from a nearby wall. The cat clutched it's heart in horror. " Is that a fire? If it is, we all can run away, but what about the vegetables?!" asked the Rooster. "True. We need to extinguish the fire! Meow!" said the cat. " If the fire comes to the garden, this entire place will be destroyed!" said the duck. " There's only one thing we can do: We must go and see what's going on for ourselves!" said Minikutty. "Go there? Where are all the other animals running away from?". Understanding their fear, Minikutty said "It's ok, don't be scared. I will go look myself!". " How!" came a chorus of confused voices. "There is a way…" Minikutty thought deeply. The other animals, not knowing what Minikutty was about to do, stared at her worriedly.

# The story of sacrifice

Suddenly, Minikutty burst out laughing and sang '

Once there was a cat,
Sleeping on a mat!
Until there came a rat,
Who wanted to have a chat.
'MEOW!' went the cat,
And tried to gobble up the rat,
Alas, for the rat,
Hid under a hat.
'Meow' said the cat,
And went back for a nap.'

Hearing this, everyone laughed (other than the cat). The doll laughed too, and guess what happened? The doll's wings activated! Minikutty jumped onto the doll's back and flew over to see what was going on. They flew above the wall and saw a family cooking food with a fire. There was a mother and father cooking food, while an old Granny washed the dishes. Nearby, there was a tiny tent made from a blue sheet. Then, the father took scooped up some food with a spoon (made from a Jackfruit leaf) to eat. He quickly ate his food, before entering the farm. " Is that my Granny's gardener?" asked Minikutty. That's when she saw a small boy coming outside the hut with a bell toy, followed by his younger sister.

The boy handed over his toy to his sister, who sang a song in Hindi.

" Amma Amma Amma Meri

Amma Amma Amma Meri

Badi Phalike Amma Meri

Thasa Dhooth Pilathi hei "


The doll realised that this was the song of people who loved their mothers most. "Those are Nomadic people" said Minikutty. " What?" questioned the doll.
"

These people will come to a place and work there for a while. They will set up these tents and live here. After a while, they remove their tent and go to another place, where they do the same. Those people are called nomads or nomadic people." Answered Minikutty.

The doll shook her head, when she noticed something. "Hey, look!" said the doll, pointing at the tent. Minikutty looked and saw the boy holding a stitched doll in his hands. "My mama!" called the doll, tears of joy streaming through her eyes. She tried to jump down towards the boy, but Minikutty held her back. " They are hugging my mama, singing to her, kissing her, showing her the birds in the trees and the sun in the sky. She is so happy there, playing with them." said the doll. Minikutty wiped the doll's tears away and said " Look, you found your mama after all! Be happy in that, for your mama is safe and sound.". The doll was crying, yet she was also smiling; like the sun peeking from behind the clouds in the monsoon season. " Look at how they bath, wipe, put powder and eyeliner, and take care of my mama" said the doll. " Don't worry, they work for Grandpa, right? I will tell him to get the doll back. You call your mother. Hearing your sound, she will be so happy, right? If not, I will call her.".

The doll sat thinking. " What are you thinking about doll?". " I don't want to take my mother" said the doll. " WHAT?!" said Minikutty, shocked. The doll rested her head against Minikutty's lap and said in a feeble voice, " Look at how the children love and take care of my mother, and look at how my mother loves them back. If- if I take my mother away from them, how can they withstand the pain and sadness?" . Minikutty was astounded. After all of this; the pain; the songs ;the adventures; the laughter, the doll was going to leave her mama for those children? " Are you sure" Minikutty asked again. "Yes. Let my mama be with them. After all, she might not be with me, but she will always be in my heart. I cannot bear it if I made them sad, for my own happiness. It might hurt me a little, but that's ok.

My mama once said not to make others sad. Let my mama forget everything and live with those children if it makes them and her happy. If she is happy, then I will also be happy." Said the doll. From bellow, the sounds of the children singing drifted upwards.

"Hear how they sing with their hearts? To them, my mother is not just a doll, but their own mother. How can I take them away from each other? Let's go now." Said the doll. Suddenly, her wings shrivelled up and fell into the floor like a bird's feather.

The words of the moon came true: *'Once you find your mama, your wings will disappear"*. Yet the doll was not sad. In fact, she was laughing! Minikutty, meanwhile, was terrified. How could they get down from the wall? A mixture of anger and sadness rose from her , and Minikutty said " Why are you laughing?". The doll looked at her friend and said " No real reason, I simply laughed!". " How can we get down from this wall? Should I call Grandpa?" said Minikutty. " No. Wait a few minutes. I want to see my mama for some more time. Then, there will be a way to climb down if we wait long enough. So the pair sat silently, not saying anything.

But far in the sky, a person was watching them. Watching the doll make the ultimate sacrifice by sacrificing its own mother for someone else's happiness. By enduring pain to see happiness on someone's else's face. The person felt the sadness inside the doll. This was what the burning, yellow, almighty Sun was thinking when it saw this! It made a decision.

# What happened next?

The one who gave her mother,
For the joy of someone else,
The one who searched hither,
For her mother, no one else.
With Golden wings and a dazzling smile,
One you could see from miles!
The doll lives happily,
With a reward for her kindness.

Seeing her sacrifice, the Sun gave the doll two rewards:

A golden, everlasting wings! She can fly anywhere and everywhere with them. All she had to do was imagine that she wanted to see her mother and smile!

The doll also could turn invisible if needed, only turning visible among her friends!

With her new powers, the doll and Minikutty lived happily ever after!

# About the translator

**Austin Ajit**

Austin Ajit is a ten-year-old child from Bangalore, India. Austin is a young naturalist, an author, an avid reader, a storyteller, and a child artist.

Austin has published five books, and this is his sixth book and the second book on translation.

1. Grandma & Austin's Plant Kingdom

2. Austin's Dino World ( Stargazer series - 1)

3. The Day I Found An Egg

4. Ammu's Earth (Translation)

5. Attack Of The Purple Blobs (Stargazer series - 2)


You can reach Austin at : austin06ajit@gmail.com

# About the author

**Unni Ammayambalam**

Unni Ammayambalam, is a Malayalam author who specialises in children's literature and has wrote over 50 interactive books for children. His books are very simple with illustrations, and the kids will be easily able to scroll through the pages. His aim is to make them understand and learn just through touch.

The author forayed into children's literature after 2002, when his book 'Mazhayathu' earned him the P T Bhaskara Panicker award for children's literature. He also bagged the State Institute for children's literature award for the best novel for his work 'Magic School Bus'. DPI poetry award for his work "Kids of Gujarath",K.M.Mathew memorial award for "Dayalu"He gained many more awards for his literary works. He works as a teacher and a co-oridnator for child helpline under central government.

www.ingramcontent.com/pod-product-compliance
Lightning Source LLC
LaVergne TN
LVHW041549070526
838199LV00046B/1882